baseball's new wave

Todd Helton

The Hits Keep Coming

By
MARK **S**TEWART

THE MILLBROOK PRESS
BROOKFIELD, CONNECTICUT

M

THE MILLBROOK PRESS

Produced by
BITTERSWEET PUBLISHING
John Sammis, President
and
TEAM STEWART, INC.
RESEARCHED AND EDITED BY MIKE KENNEDY WITH SPECIAL THANKS TO KAREN RUSSO

Series Design and Electronic Page Makeup by
JAFFE ENTERPRISES
Ron Jaffe

All photos courtesy Rich Clarkson and Associates, LLC. (© 2000) except the following:
Knoxville News-Sentinel — Pages 7, 9
University of Tennessee — Pages 10, 12, 13, 15, 16
AP/ Wide World Photos, Inc. — Pages 14, 22, 33, 40
New Haven Ravens — Page 20
The following images are from the collection of Team Stewart:
Fleer Corp. — Page 26 top (© 1988)
Upper Deck Company, LLC — Page 30 top (© 1999)
Topps Company, Inc. — Page 30 bottom (© 1999)
Fleer/Skybox International LP — Page 39 (© 2000)

Printed in the United States of America

Published by
The Millbrook Press, Inc.
2 Old New Milford Road
Brookfield, Connecticut   06804

www.millbrookpress.com

Library of Congress Cataloging-in-Publication Data

Stewart, Mark.
   Todd Helton : the hits keep coming / by Mark Stewart.
      p. cm. – (Baseball's new wave)
   Includes index.
   ISBN 0-7613-2271-X (lib. bdg.)
      1. Helton, Todd—Juvenile literature. 2. Baseball players—United States—
   Biography—Juvenile literature. [1. Helton, Todd. 2. Baseball players.] I. Title:
   Helton. II. Title. III. Series.

   GV865.H44 S74 2001
   796.357'092—dc21
   [B]
                                                                    00-065395

1 3 5 7 9 10 8 6 4 2

Contents

Practice Makes Perfect

chapter 1

"He was a good kid but he was strong-willed. He knew what he wanted and he knew how to get it."

— MARTHA HELTON

Some kids just seem a lot older than they really are. Everyone knows someone like that—someone who is a little taller, a little stronger, a little smarter, and a little cooler than the other kids in their class. Todd Helton was like that when he was a kid. In fact, that is what most of his childhood friends remember about him. Todd was born in the summer of 1973, and grew up in the city of Knoxville, Tennessee. He was the second of three children born to Jerry and Martha Helton.

Some say Todd is the "best of both" parents, and it would be hard to argue with that. Jerry was a big, strong young man who was well known around Knoxville in his youth. He earned All-State honors in football (as a running back) and baseball (as a catcher), and was a very good hockey player, too. After Jerry's high-school graduation

Todd Helton says his parents taught him two important things: "You have to work hard for everything... and it's probably not worth anything if you don't have to work for it."

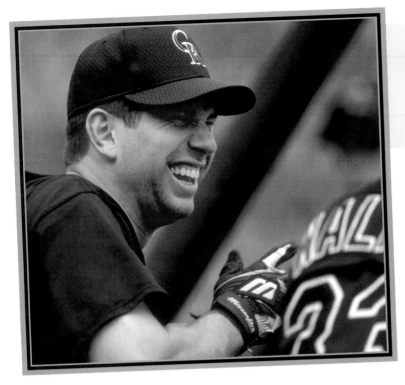

he signed a contract with the Minnesota Twins to play minor-league baseball. Martha was a calm, intelligent, and highly focused person who believed that brainpower could solve just about any problem. Her father, Don Ferguson, was the head of the Chemical Technology division of Oak Ridge National Laboratories. A brilliant scientist, he had worked on the first atomic bomb in the 1940s.

"Todd got his grit and determination from the Heltons," Todd's father claims, "but his coolness under pressure came from Don."

These qualities made Todd one of the best athletes in his neighborhood. When he was little, his older brother, Rodney, would take him along to baseball, basketball, and football games and make sure he got a chance to play. Soon, Todd was one of the first kids picked. The sport he liked most of all, however, was fishing. He and his friends would take their bikes down to a spot they called "Big Foot" and fish for hours. Later, in high school, Todd often slept at his grandparents' house, so he could go fishing before school. Their house was right on a lake.

Todd's second-favorite sport was baseball. He loved to hit. When Todd was five years old, his father set up a tiny batting cage in the family basement. He would throw pitches to Todd, and call out where he wanted the boy to hit them. Todd wanted to pull everything, but his father told him it was more important to drive the ball up the middle and to the opposite field. Todd would develop a great stroke, his father promised.

Todd was good enough in high school to be drafted as a pitcher.

In between batting and fielding drills, Todd did agility drills to improve his balance and foot-work. Not surprisingly, starting at the age of six, Todd was the best hitter in every league he joined, right up through high school.

Jerry Helton told Todd, Rodney, and their sister, Melissa, that he did not care what sport they liked to play or what activity they liked to do, as long as they tried to do the best they could. The same went for schoolwork—if you take a class, give it 100 percent. "You don't go to school to make Cs," he would say to them. "Cs are average, and you never want to be average."

Todd took this message to heart. It made every day a challenge, and he liked challenges. "I've always been a goal-oriented person," he says. "Not just in sports, but in life. What do you have to look forward to, or strive for, if you don't have goals, something to make you better?"

In school, Todd was a favorite of all the teachers. He got his homework done, raised his hand a lot, and did especially well on tests and quizzes. Only once, in fact, did he get less than an A in a class. In sports, his give-it-all-you've-got approach made him one of the best baseball and football players in the city. It also put a lot of pressure on his father. Almost every evening, Jerry Helton would come home from work to find young Todd waiting for him in the living room, with a ball in his hands. "You ready, Dad?" he would ask.

Jerry was always ready. He wanted his children to enjoy sports as much as he did. Still, he was careful not to be too pushy. The Helton kids got advice only when they asked for it. "But as soon as you'd ask him, he was ready," says Todd.

By the time Todd was a freshman in high school, Rodney had already gone off to college. The University of Alabama offered him a scholarship, and he accepted, playing for Coach Bill Curry along with future NFL stars Derrick Thomas and Bobby Humphrey. Todd thought about following in his brother's footsteps. A year earlier, he quit basketball so he could focus more on football and baseball. He knew in the coming years he might have to choose between these two sports.

If given the choice, Todd would have selected baseball. But during his four years at Knox Central High, he was so good at both sports—and did so well in school—that no one ever made him choose. He was the best pitcher and hitter on the baseball team, and the starting quarterback and star defensive back on the football team.

Did You Know?

In 1968, Jerry Helton was a minor-league teammate of future major leaguers Steve Brye and Ray Corbin. In 1970, the Twins invited Jerry to big-league training camp. He did not make the team, and was sent back to the minors. Instead of reporting, he quit baseball and returned to Knoxville. Todd's brother Rodney had been born the year before, and Jerry needed to make more money. He got a job as a salesman.

As a senior, Todd ran and threw for a combined 2,458 yards, intercepted 7 passes, and scored a total of 33 touchdowns. In baseball, he batted .655, hit 10 home runs, knocked in 35 runs and made just 27 outs all season. He was voted Player of the Year for his region in both sports, and was named Scholar Athlete of the Year by the National Football Foundation. Baseball America selected him to its High-School All-America team.

Todd prepares to hand off during a game in his senior year. The footwork he mastered as a quarterback now helps him around first base.

Every college in the country wanted Todd. He was a once-in-a-lifetime athlete with a 3.93 grade point average. The scholarship offers rolled in, but Todd knew exactly where he wanted to go. The same place every kid in Knoxville dreams about: The University of Tennessee.

*Todd turned down an offer from the Padres and chose to wear
the orange and white of the Tennessee Volunteers.*

Player's Choice

chapter 1

"If he'd wanted to play football,
I think he would have been a
Dan Marino-type quarterback."

— JERRY HELTON

On June 1, 1992, the phone rang at the Helton home. It was a representative from the San Diego Padres baseball team. Todd had been selected in the second round of the Major League draft. Todd was very tempted to try pro baseball, especially when the Padres offered him a signing bonus of $450,000—the largest ever offered to a second-round pick at the time. "It was something I always wanted to do," Todd remembers.

At this point, Todd's grandparents sat down with him and tried to explain how important it was to get an education. His parents wanted him to go to college, too. His father told him about how tough the minors could be on a teenager, and how great it would be to become a college quarterback. Jerry Helton said he would not sign the contract for Todd (who was technically a minor, still just 17). To this day, Todd believes his mother would have signed for him had he asked her, but he knew she did not want him to play ball, so he never asked.

Todd rolls out and looks for a receiver. He enjoyed playing in games, but hated the practices.

Todd took everyone's advice and turned down San Diego's offer. Some thought it might be a negotiating trick to get more money out of the Padres, but Todd says definitely not. "Money wasn't an issue," he explains. "There were some circumstances with my family that made it not feel right."

The problem was that football did not feel right, either. He had never loved the sport the way he loved baseball. He was just really good at it. Tennessee coach Phil Fulmer was thrilled to have Todd. He planned to make him a backup to Heath Shuler, and then develop him into the team's starter. Todd was flattered, but after a couple of practices he thought he had made a horrible mistake. "I thought, this is for the birds," he laughs. "I called the Padres back and told them I wanted to sign, to come out and we'd discuss it."

After placing the call, Todd told his father he had reopened negotiations with San Diego. His dad begged him not to make the same mistake he had. He assured Todd that if he was good enough, he would get another chance to play pro ball. In the end, Todd stuck with Tennessee.

"It's not that I didn't like football," Todd explains. "I really enjoyed high-school football, but I didn't really enjoy college football. I liked to play the games, but I didn't like the practice. In baseball, I enjoy the practice almost as much as the games."

The other thing that worried Todd was that, to develop into a big-time college quarterback, he might have to turn his back on baseball. "I felt the other guys had an advantage on me," he says of the other quarterbacks. "They were working year-round and I was playing baseball."

Well, no matter how great his potential in football, there was no way he was going to quit baseball. "I knew I wasn't going to be the quarterback for long," he sighs. "While I played, I just tried my best."

Todd's best, it turned out, was good enough to win the starting job. After seeing limited action in 1992 and 1993, he was promoted seven plays into the 1994 season, when senior Jerry Colquitt hurt his knee in the season opener. By then, however, Todd sensed that his time as the starter would be short. Tennessee had a weak team and a freshman on the bench named Peyton Manning.

Manning was the best quarterback Todd had ever seen. The son of a former NFL passer, he came to school look-ing more like a pro than a high-schooler. When it became clear that the Volunteers were going nowhere, it was only a matter of time before Manning would get a chance to play. When Todd twisted a knee in his fourth start, he knew his foot-ball days were coming to an end. "It was watching Manning that I realized in a hurry that football was not in my future," he says.

Most quarterbacks who see their careers come to an end are depressed. Todd, however, could not have been happier. Although college football was a

As a freshman, Todd played first base and also won six games as a pitcher.

Todd thought it was very exciting when Cuba's star shortstop, Rey Ordoñez, defected during a tournament in Buffalo, New York.

drag, college itself was a blast! Todd had made the baseball team as a freshman and quickly became the team's most valuable player. He batted .348 with 11 homers and finished third in the Southeastern Conference (SEC) with 66 RBIs. He made the SEC All-Conference team, and was voted to the Freshman All-America team. When Coach Rob Delmonico needed a clutch hit, Todd usually delivered it. When he needed a clutch pitching performance, he could call on Todd, too. The freshman won six games, working both as a starter and reliever. Tennessee finished with the best record in the SEC.

Todd's second year was even better. He hit .355 and drove home 80 runs to establish a new school record and lead the SEC. He also had the lowest ERA of any pitcher at 0.89. Every other game or so, when Tennessee was in a tight spot during the late innings, Coach Delmonico would summon Todd from his position at first base, hand him the ball, and tell him to "seal the deal." Todd responded with 5 wins, 11 saves, and 51 strikeouts in 50 innings. Once again, he received All-America honors, and once again the Volunteers finished with the SEC's best record.

That summer, Todd was selected to play for Team USA. The team competed against amateur squads from other nations, and participated in the World University games in Buffalo, New York, and the International Cup, which was held in Italy. The United States was runner-up to Cuba in Italy, marking the first time in five summers that an American team had reached the finals of a major event.

There was no lack of excitement that summer. In Buffalo, two Cuban players defected, including shortstop Rey Ordoñez, whose eye-popping fielding plays made him a major sensation. In an August tournament in Nicaragua, fans mobbed the team bus looking for souvenirs, nearly starting a riot. Todd missed that trip because he had to report to school for football practice. Though he missed the squad's final event, Todd had a lot of fun and played very well. He batted a team-high .352 and was fourth on the national squad in hits and RBIs.

Did You Know?

Todd hoped to major in veterinary medicine when he enrolled at Tennessee. "But in my first day in chemistry class, I knew this was going to be too time-consuming if I was going to play two sports. So I switched very quickly to business management."

Although Todd would become one of the biggest stars in college sports, his fondest memory of his college days has nothing to do with sports. It took place in a freshman biology class, where he shared a microscope with a girl named Kristi Bollman. "We met looking into a lens together at a dissected frog," he says.

After a while, Todd mustered the courage to ask her to go out on a date with him. A soccer player, Kristi had seen Todd at one of her games, and had also run into him at a party. Since she was from Chattanooga, in the western part of the state, she had no idea that Todd was a big local hero. He seemed nice, so she agreed to make a date.

A few days later, Kristi was watching the Tennessee football game at her brother-in-law's house and the announcers started talking about Todd. "Hey," she said. "That's the guy who asked me out."

Eight years later Todd and Kristi were married.

Did You Know?

Todd's teammates during his first year with the Tennessee baseball team included Bubba Trammell, whom he later faced when Bubba was a member of the New York Mets.

Dream Seasons

chapter }

"Things like that are never going to happen again."

—TODD HELTON

By the spring of his junior year, Todd had put football behind him. He was totally focused on baseball, and it definitely showed. Todd turned in one of the greatest seasons in the history of college baseball. He batted .407 with 20 home runs and 92 RBIs, coming within one hit of winning the SEC's triple crown. As it was, Todd led the conference in hits, runs, doubles, RBIs, and slugging percentage—and once again he had the lowest ERA. He won 8 games and saved 12 more to contribute to more than a third of Tennessee's 54 victories. Four times during the 1995 season, Coach Delmonico asked Todd to give his starters a rest and start a game himself. Four times he took the ball and turned in a complete-game victory.

Todd had a monster year at the plate for Tennessee in 1995, and also had the lowest ERA in the SEC.

*Tennessee coach
Rob Delmonico*

Before Todd came along, the Tennessee baseball program had been the laughingstock of the SEC. By the end of his junior year, it was the most feared. That spring, for the first time in four years, the Volunteers were invited to participate in the College World Series. Everyone was saying that Todd had saved Tennessee baseball. He insists he did nothing of the sort. Todd says the credit for Tennessee's turnaround belongs to Delmonico, who brought in a winning attitude. He claims he just came to play ball and have fun. And that's all he did. "I just wanted to come in and play as hard as I could," he says. "I wanted to set an example, play the game the way I thought it should be played."

Todd considers his junior year at Tennessee as close to perfect as a year could be. He got a chance to start for the football team before Peyton Manning took over, then won every baseball award in sight in the spring. He also got to hang out with Rodney, who shared an apartment with him. "That was definitely the best year of my life," Todd maintains. "I was living with my brother and got to spend a lot of time with him. I got to play some football and had a great year in baseball."

college *stats*

Year	School	H	R	2B	HR	RBI	BA
1993	Tennessee	86	48	22	11	66	.348
1994	Tennessee	89	65	16	7	80*	.355
1995	Tennessee	105*	86*	27*	20*	92*	.407

Year	School	G	IP	W	L	SV	K	ERA
1993	Tennessee	14	67	6	3	0	47	3.92
1994	Tennessee	28	50	5	0	11	51	0.89*
1995	Tennessee	30	76	8	2	12	74	1.66*

* LED SEC

college *highlights*

Freshman All-American 1993

First-Team All-SEC 1993–95

SEC Tournament MVP 1993–95

First-Team All-American 1994–95

SEC Athlete of the Year 1995

Baseball America Player of the Year 1995

Todd was selected eighth in the 1995 draft by the Colorado Rockies. The team gave him a big bonus and assigned him to its Class-A club in Asheville, North Carolina, just a couple of hours from home. Todd joined a team that featured Colorado's top prospect, Derrick Gibson. Gibson was well on his way to a monster season when Todd joined the Tourists in July. Batting in front of Gibson, he saw plenty of good pitches, but was unable to continue his college success. Part of the problem was that he had gone almost two months without playing in a game. Also, he was using heavy wood bats instead of the lightweight aluminum ones allowed in college. "I was expecting to go out there and tear it up," Todd says. "And I didn't. I had some bad times."

"I got enough 'humble pie' that year to last my career," Todd remembers. "I think more than anything I was tired, mentally and physically, before I walked into my first professional summer."

Todd in action during his first full season as a pro with the New Haven Ravens

Dick Balderson, in charge of personnel for the Rockies, believed that stationing Todd so close to home had been a mistake. He needed to be by himself for a change. That fall, the team sent him to play in a developmental league in Hawaii, where he hit .291 against high-caliber pitching.

In 1996, Todd was moved up a level to the Class-AA New Haven Ravens. There he finally adjusted to wood bats and began pulling the ball for power. In 93 games he pounded out 33 extra-base hits and recorded a .332 batting average. Todd was named to the Eastern League All-Star team, and won the All-Star game with a tie-breaking home run. It was one of the hardest and longest balls he had hit in his life, and ESPN ran videotape of the blast for several days. With a month left in the 1996 season Todd

Andres Galarraga gives Todd pointers on playing first base. The "Big Cat" knew Todd would one day take his job away.

earned a promotion to Class-AAA Colorado Springs. He continued to hammer the ball, batting .352 in 21 games.

Todd began thinking about making the Rockies. He had done well at every level in the minors, and had a perfect swing for Denver's Coors Field. The only problem was that the National League's top power hitter, Andres Galarraga, was the Colorado first baseman. The "Big Cat" had led the National League (N.L.) with 47 home runs and 150 RBIs in 1996, and he fielded his position beautifully.

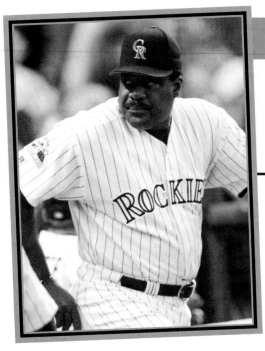

During spring training, Todd and Andres stood next to each other in fielding drills, alternating with each batted ball. Galarraga knew Todd was there to take his position, but helped him with his defense anyway. The millionaire superstar did not even mind when Todd produced four multihit games while he sat on the bench with a sore hamstring. Galarraga is one of baseball's nicest people. "If I stay in the game that long and make that kind of money," Todd jokes, "I'll be a nice guy, too!"

Although everyone on the Rockies agreed that Todd was already a good major-league hitter, the team sent him back to the minors so he could play every day.

minor league *stats*

Year	Team	G	H	R	2B	HR	RBI	BA
1995	Asheville	54	51	24	11	1	15	.254
1996	New Haven	93	106	46	24	7	51	.332
	CO Springs	21	25	13	4	2	13	.352
1997	CO Springs	99	138	87	31	16	88	.352

minor league *highlights*

Eastern League All-Star	1996
Pacific Coast League All-Star	1997

Cracking the Lineup

chapter 4

"There's no telling what he can accomplish, because he's an extraordinary talent."

— CLINT HURDLE, ROCKIES
BATTING COACH

The Colorado Rockies were confident that Todd could handle major-league pitching. Before they gave him a chance to play first base in the majors, however, he would have to prove he could pick out pitches over the inside part of home plate and drive them for home runs. Playing in 99 games for the Colorado Springs Sky Sox, Todd belted 16 homers while keeping his average above .350.

As the season progressed, the Rockies realized they had to find a place for Todd in the majors. Orders

Did You Know?

Early in the 1998 season, Manager Don Baylor "protected" Todd by benching him against tough lefties and playing Greg Colbrunn at first base. "When you have young kids, too often they are thrown out there to sink or swim," says Baylor, "and some guys drown. Todd was so gifted, I didn't want that to happen to him." Soon Todd was hitting against all pitchers, and ended up batting .304 against lefthanders for the year.

Neifi Perez hangs tough turning a double play. He and Todd were the two players the Rockies planned to build around.

were issued to Manager Paul Zuvella to have Todd start playing left field. It felt strange to play a new position, but by early August he was doing well enough to earn a call-up to Colorado. Todd played in 35 games and hit .280 with 5 home runs. He played left field, first base, and joined veteran John Vanderwal to give the Rockies the league's best left-handed pinch-hitting duo.

The Rockies looked past Todd's numbers and saw even more to like. He did something that is unusual for a young hitter: He changed his approach depending on the game situation, knowing that the pitcher would pitch him differently. He also showed no fear of hitting with two strikes. Todd knew the pitching would be tough in the

Did You Know?

As a rookie, Todd began keeping a detailed notebook on pitchers. He wrote down what different pitchers did to get him out. After facing the same pitcher a few times, he could usually pick up patterns in the way he worked him. By the end of the year, he had the upper hand on almost every hurler in the league.

majors, but was confident that he could deal with it. "Pitching is the biggest difference up here," he confirms. "Nothing is straight. Everything cuts, runs, sinks, rises, or something. It's a matter of learning to trust the plan you take up to the plate and not changing it after you get a strike."

What the Rockies liked most of all was Todd's attitude. He was serious about baseball. In fact, they were afraid he was a bit *too* serious. "When I first came up to the majors and I'd have a bad day, I'd punish myself," Todd remembers. "I would do something like not eat dinner. Now I've come to appreciate that we play 162 games a year, and you're going to *have* bad days. And not eating dinner hurts, it doesn't help."

Over the winter, the team decided not to re-sign Andres Galarraga, who had become a free agent. That meant Todd came to camp in the spring of 1998 knowing the first-base job was his. Years earlier, the Rockies had invested in young players like Todd. Now these players were beginning to reach the majors and replace the team's

Amazing
Grace

Todd chose uniform number 17 because his favorite player, Mark Grace, wears it. "I like the way Gracie plays," says Todd, "all-out with a full-range game."

"Todd is going to be a whole lot better player than I ever was," Grace says. "He's got a great talent and a great attitude. He's not like a lot of guys today."

Todd was just 14 when Grace's rookie card came out. Now the two first basemen are good friends.

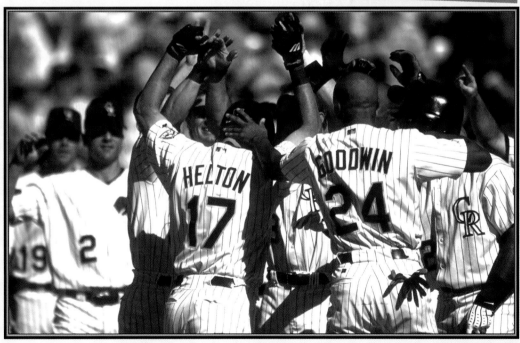

Todd handled first base well in his first full season as a major leaguer.

older stars. The first was shortstop Neifi Perez, a teammate of Todd's in the minors who had taken over at shortstop from Walt Weiss midway through the 1997 season.

Colorado's veterans included sluggers Vinny Castilla, Larry Walker, Ellis Burks, and Dante Bichette. With this quartet carrying the load on offense, Todd and the other young Rockies could develop at their own pace without too much pressure. The fans were also excited about the pitching, which had long been a problem. Nineteen-game winner Darryl Kile had joined the club as a free agent, giving the Rockies the first true "ace" in their history.

Replacing a player as popular as Galarraga is a very hard thing to do. Todd found out just *how* hard when, during the season's first 30 games, he batted just .250 and

> "I think everyone knows what Todd Helton is made of. He could easily have crumbled to the pressure. But he just kept plowing away."
>
> **FORMER GM BOB GEBHARD**

failed to hit a home run. Galarraga, meanwhile, was hitting homers like crazy and the Braves were building a big league in the N.L. East. Every time Todd opened a newspaper or turned on the radio, someone was saying the Rockies had made a horrible mistake. "I was worried about getting sent down," Todd admits.

Slowly but surely, Todd turned his season around. By the end of May, his average had climbed to .285. By the end of July he had 17 home runs. In August, Todd led all National Leaguers with a .398 average. And in the season's final month he again topped the .300 mark. The difference? Gaining experience, and building confidence. "I figured out that maybe I do belong here," Todd remembers. "You can say you belong all you want, but until you go out there and do the job every day, you're just saying it—you don't believe it."

Batting sixth or seventh most of the year, Todd found Coors Field to his liking and batted a robust .354 at home. The ball carried well in Denver's thin air, so many of the line drives he hit rattled off the outfield fence or flew over it. When Todd saw out-

Manager Jim Leyland took over as Rockies manager in 1999.

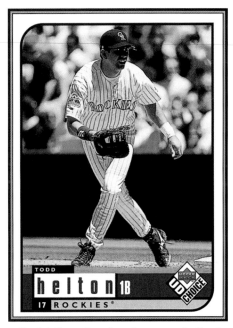

Todd likes the trading cards that show him fielding as much as the ones that picture him swinging. Defense, he says, is an important part of his all-around game.

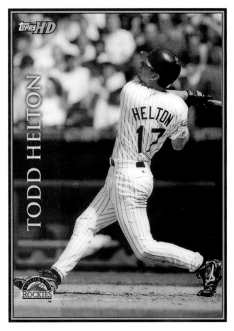

fielders playing him deep, he simply dumped the ball in front of them for easy singles. Pitchers sometimes tried to tempt Todd into swinging at bad pitches, but he rarely made this kind of "rookie" mistake. He was so patient, in fact, that he walked as many times as he struck out.

Todd completed his first full major-league season with 25 home runs, 97 RBIs, and a batting average of .315. He batted .386 with runners in scoring position, which led the team. The most impressive statistic from Todd's rookie year was that he batted above .300 against both righties and lefties. Most players go their entire lives without accomplishing this.

Todd finished second to Cubs pitcher Kerry Wood in the closest Rookie of the Year race in 16 years. The Rockies were so happy with Todd that they tore up his contract after the season and signed him to a four-year, $12 million deal.

The team hoped Todd would help erase the memory of what had been an otherwise disappointing 1998 season. Back in April, it appeared as if the Rockies and Los Angeles Dodgers would be battling for the Western Division title. But by midsummer, the San Diego Padres were way out in front. By the time the Padres cooled off, it was too late for the Rockies to catch them. Walker and Burks battled injuries, and not one of the starters won as many games as he lost. Colorado finished fourth, with a 77–85 record.

The 1999 season looked a lot more promising. Colorado broke camp that spring with pretty much the same team it had the year before.

However, the veterans were healthy, the youngsters a year older, and the manager was now Jim Leyland, one of the brightest skippers in baseball. One of Leyland's first moves was to shift Todd into the middle of the batting order, where he would see better pitches and get a chance to hit with more men on base.

Todd responded with another good season, producing 35 home runs, 113 RBIs, and a .320 average. Walker, Bichette, and Castilla each had more than 30 homers and 100 RBIs, too. But the team failed to hit in the clutch, and the pitching staff could not hold a lead. Despite having more talent than many of its rivals, Colorado finished dead last with a record of 72–90.

Once again, the team got off to a slow start and never climbed back into the race. Todd started slowly, too, and did not get his average up over .300 until well after the All-Star break. After that, he was fantastic. But it was too little, too late.

In this lost year for the Rockies, Todd was able to make some important gains. He perfected his home-run swing, and was now able to yank inside pitches right down the line and into the seats. This meant that opponents had to think twice before attempting to jam him. Also, Todd's "book" on pitchers was really paying off. Hurlers around the league now knew that they could not get him out the same way twice in a row. This meant that pitchers had to use their second- or third-best pitches against Todd, who usually crushed them.

By the end of his second full season, Todd was ready to assume his place among baseball's elite players.

The Helton File

TODD'S FAVORITE...

Food . . . . Spaghetti
Singer . . . . George Strait
Book . . . . *Kiss the Girls*
by James Patterson
Way to Relax . . Playing video games
Hall of Famer . . . . Rod Carew
City to Visit . . . . . . Houston, Texas
Dog . . . . Chocolate Lab

A natural leader, Todd was elected by his teammates as their player representative in 1998—the first time that a rookie was ever asked to fill that role.

Chasing History

chapter 5

"I've prepared my whole life for this. This is what it's all about."

—TODD HELTON

bility, confidence, concentration—in baseball, if you have these three things you can do almost anything. To hit .400 for an entire season, however, you also need a little help. Not since 1941, when Ted Williams batted .406, has a player accomplished this feat. Williams, who was perhaps the best pure hitter baseball has ever known, reached the .400 level at a time when African-American players were banned from the majors. Would he have had as many hits facing Satchel Paige and Leon Day, the star pitchers of the Negro National League?

Did You Know?

The last player to make a serious run at .400 was Hall of Famer George Brett, who ended up with a .390 average. "George was the greatest hitter I ever saw," says Colorado manager Buddy Bell, "and he couldn't hit .400, so that should tell you something about how hard it is."

Rogers Hornsby (left) and Ty Cobb (right) each batted over .400 three times. Cobb hit .401 at the age of 34.

Earlier players who hit .400, such as all-time greats Ty Cobb and Rogers Hornsby, did so in an era when relief-pitching specialists were unknown. In the late innings, they often faced exhausted hurlers trying desperately to finish what they started. How many hits might they have lost trying to catch up to the 95 miles (153 kilometers) per hour fastballs that today's players see in the eighth and ninth innings?

When Todd Helton made it through the first two months of the 2000 season with a batting average close to .400, the experts began to evaluate his chances of hitting .400 for the entire year. Todd certainly possessed the talent and consistency to produce line drives week after week. He had demonstrated his ability to analyze how opponents were getting him out, and then make the correct adjustments. He had extraordinary concentration, and as an ex-quarterback he knew how to ignore the aches and pains of playing and get results. Something else Todd had going for him was the position he played. First base requires good reactions and quick feet, but it does not wear down an athlete the way shortstop or outfield does. It looked like Todd had a really good chance!

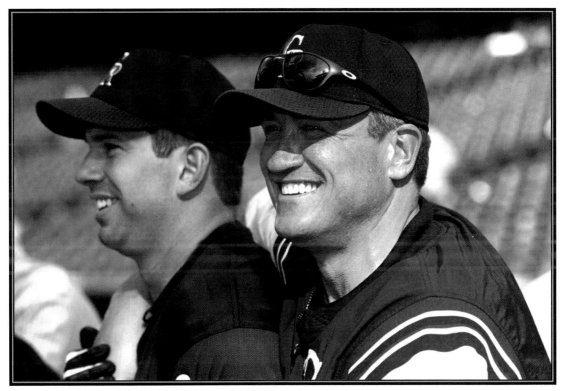

Todd and Coach Clint Hurdle share a laugh during pregame warm-ups.

The biggest thing Todd had in his favor was his home ballpark. Coors Field's thin atmosphere turned long outs into home runs, yet its actual dimensions were quite large. This left a lot of room for line drives to drop in between and in front of the outfielders. In other words, it was a perfect place for Todd to get the extra help he would need to reach the .400 plateau. "Is it a good park to hit in?" says Todd, a bit defensively. "Yeah. So are Wrigley Field and Camden Yards. I didn't design Coors Field—I just play there."

The difference between a .350 hitter and a .400 hitter is roughly 35 hits (less than two more hits a week). Would the Coors advantage be enough for Todd? For most of the 2000 season, this was the question on everyone's mind.

Actually, Todd's quest to be the first .400 hitter in 59 years began the season before. Prior to an August game against the Milwaukee Brewers, he and batting coach Clint Hurdle had a talk. For the second year in a row, the Rockies had fallen short of expec-

Hitter-friendly Coors Field

Todd watches one of his league-leading 216 hits during the 2000 season

tations. Manager Jim Leyland had given up (he would be replaced by Buddy Bell in 2000), and many of the players had, too. Todd loved baseball, but Hurdle could see that walking into the clubhouse was no longer fun for him. Fearing that his young pupil would let the season slip away, Hurdle asked him if he would be willing to try a little experiment.

The difference between a typical major-league hitter and a superstar, said Hurdle, has less to do with skill than it does with attitude. Most guys step into the batter's box hoping to get a hit. A select few—the ones opponents truly fear—step into the batter's box looking to do serious damage to the other team. The secret, he told Todd, is in "the walk." You let a pitcher know you're locked in

"You've got to walk from that dugout knowing you're going to put a good swing on a good pitch and you're going to hit the ball hard. You walk from the dugout to the on-deck circle and every time a pitcher looks on-deck, you should be looking at him. You don't let him breathe."

CLINT HURDLE

from the moment you grab a bat. You carry the bat like a weapon. You're a *warrior*. You let the pitcher know you're bringing your best to the plate, and anything less than *his* best won't be enough.

"It was one of the best speeches I've ever been given," says Todd. "And I've been given a lot of good ones."

Todd worked on "the walk" in the final weeks of the 1999 season, and continued to think about it over the winter and during spring training in 2000. He got so into perfecting his icy glare and menacing swagger that for a time he forgot about his mechanics at the plate. Indeed, when the 2000 season started, Todd was dropping his left shoulder and uppercutting the ball. The walk must have been working, however, because by the time he and Hurdle ironed out his swing, he was batting well over .300!

Around the end of April, Todd finally got comfortable. During a six-game homestand, he hit .625 to bring his average up around the .400 mark. In one of those games,

Todd slides into third base after legging out a triple. His 103 extra-base hits in 2000 were the most by a National Leaguer since 1948.

Todd hit 3 home runs and knocked in 9 runs. At the end of May, Todd went on a 13-for-20 tear.

The fans did not realize it, but Todd was doing all this damage with another player's bats. Utility player Jeff Manto used 32-ounce, 34.5-inch Louisville Slugger bats. Although the ones the company made for Todd were the same weight and similar in length, Manto's just felt better to Todd. Manto, who only got a couple of swings a week, was happy to let Todd use his bats. A problem arose, however, when Manto was sent to the minors. Louisville Slugger would not send "Manto bats" to Todd in Denver, so *Jeff* had to send the bats to Todd! "Have you ever heard of a guy in Triple-A sending bats to a guy in the big leagues?" Todd laughs.

Then Manto was traded to the Cleveland organization! It looked like that was that for the bats. Todd cracked the last one in July and went back to his own model. After a weeklong slump, however, Todd panicked. "Finally, I said, 'I've got to get some more Jeff Manto bats,'" Todd remembers. "I called him and said, 'Send 'em!'"

Todd's hitting reignited, and through July and August he stayed right at .400, with his average climbing as high as .417. Needless to say, his confidence was sky-high. He especially noticed how good he felt in late-inning situations. When he first came to the majors, Todd would psyche himself out

Did You Know?

Todd and Clint Hurdle have a lot in common. Both were multisport stars in high school, both were recruited to play quarterback for major college football programs, and both were labeled "can't-miss" prospects when they came to the majors. The chief difference is that Hurdle tried to live up to the hype, and it destroyed him. His job is to keep Todd from making the same mistake. "I tried to please everyone," Hurdle remembers, "and ended up pleasing no one. I've seen the game's negative side and try to make Todd aware of that."

Todd follows the flight of a home run. He hit 42 during the 2000 season.

when the other team's "closer" came into the game. "I'd think, 'I'm not going to hit this guy,'" he admits. "Now I go up thinking, 'You'd better not throw a strike!'"

By the beginning of September, Todd's average had dipped into the .390s. He was still stinging the ball, but several of his hits went directly at fielders. Earlier in the season, the same hits seemed to "find" holes and drop in. Todd's quest for .400 ended at .372, proving just how hard it is to accomplish this feat. His final numbers, however, put him in some impressive company. Only four other players in history have done what Todd did in 2000: 200 hits, 40 homers, 100 RBIs, 100 extra-base hits, and 100 walks. Their names are Babe Ruth, Lou Gehrig, Hank Greenberg, and Jimmie Foxx—each a Hall of Famer.

Todd's season ranks among the greatest ever. He batted .372 to lead the major leagues in hitting, beating out Nomar Garciaparra by one one-thousandth of a point! He led the National League in slugging (.698), RBIs (147), and doubles (59). His 59 two-base hits were the most by a player since World War II, and only 8 off the all-time record. His average was the highest by a first baseman since 1930.

Todd was proud of his performance in 2000, but disappointed in his team's finish. For most of the year, the division was up for grabs. At the All-Star break, the Rockies were just a couple of wins behind the Arizona Diamondbacks. But an 11-game losing streak took them out of the running. Although the Rockies finished with a winning record, they were 15 games in back of the division-winning San Francisco Giants.

Todd (right) credits Jeff Cirillo (left) and Jeffrey Hammonds (center) with "protecting" him in the Colorado lineup during the 2000 season. Each player enjoyed the best year of his career.

major league *stats*

Year	Team	G	H	R	2B	HR	RBI	BA
1997	Rockies	35	26	13	2	5	11	.280
1998	Rockies	152	167	78	37	25	97	.315
1999	Rockies	159	185	114	39	35	113	.320
2000	Rockies	160	216*	138	59*	42	147*	.372*
TOTAL		**506**	**594**	**343**	**137**	**107**	**368**	**.334**

* LED NATIONAL LEAGUE

major league *highlights*

Rookie of the Year Runner-Up 1998
N.L. Assists Leader 1998, 2000
N.L. All-Star 2000

Working For a Living

chapter 6

"He's always had leadership tendencies, but now he seems louder, more like the quarterback of the clubhouse."

—JERRY DiPOTO, TEAMMATE

Only one team in each league can make it to the World Series, which leaves a lot of disappointed players every October. Todd has learned to look for the silver lining in this dark cloud. The youth movement that began when he and Neifi Perez came to the majors in 1997 is now complete. When team management realized it had no chance to win the division in 2000, it got rid of some older players and brought in new ones.

The heart of the team going into 2001 was Todd, Larry Walker, and Jeff Cirillo, the hot-hitting third baseman acquired from the Brewers. Surrounding them is a group of young players on the rise, including catcher Ben Petrick, outfielder Juan Pierre, and

Todd's experience as a quarterback makes plays like this one easy.
Give him a helmet and pads, and he could be pitching out to a running back!

Todd is as much a Denver landmark now as the city skyline.

two more Todds—Todd Hollandsworth and Todd Walker. Other pieces of the puzzle will follow, and perhaps very soon Todd Helton will become the centerpiece of a pennant contender.

When you are a baseball player, part of looking ahead requires you to look back. You have to learn from your mistakes, of course, but you must understand what you have done right, too. Todd learned some valuable lessons from his wonderful 2000 season. He had set reachable goals for himself—"start off better, hit lefties better, hit on the road better"—and he accomplished all of these things.

Todd's great start actually took root during the winter, when he and personal trainer Charles Petrone designed a workout he could follow at home in Knoxville. Instead of bulking up, as many young players try to do, Todd concentrated on flexibility. This helped him avoid injuries and make adjustments from game to game, and even swing to swing.

Improving his stats against lefthanders was a simple matter of taking extra batting practice from lefthanded pitchers. In 1999, Todd hit lefties for a meager .245 average. In 2000, he improved to .329! And by adjusting his approach to the different ballparks the Rockies visited—just as he does at home in Colorado—Todd raised his away average from .252 in 1999 to .353. Those who claimed that he was just a "Coors Field hitter" were forced to eat their words.

Todd developed in other important ways during 2000. Larry Walker, an MVP and batting champion, was the team's undisputed leader when Todd first came to the club. Walker missed nearly two months of the 2000 season because of an elbow injury. This cost the Rockies some wins, but it gave Todd a chance to step up and assume a leadership role. It felt like his old football days at Tennessee, when he was in charge of the huddle. The Colorado clubhouse, which was a tense place during Todd's first few seasons, is now a great place to come to every day. Todd had a lot to do with that.

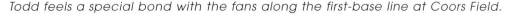

Todd feels a special bond with the fans along the first-base line at Coors Field.

"When you talk about role models and what athletes should be, a person like Todd Helton is good for baseball."

GM DAN O'DOWD

Can Todd continue to improve? Can he put up crazy numbers every year? Can he take the Rockies all the way to the World Series? There may be no player in baseball who is better suited to perform this task. For although Todd has tons of natural ability, you will never see him rely on that ability. He takes nothing for granted. Every day Todd comes to the ballpark, he is dreaming up ways to beat the other team. And then he goes to the film room, the weight room, or the batting cage to perfect this new strategy. "I'm a grinder," Todd says. "I have to grind. I have to work at this game."

Todd Helton is on track for a historic career. Nothing, it seems, can derail him—unless the hard work it takes to be a star becomes boring. According to Todd, that will never happen. Because the *work* is what he has always enjoyed most about baseball.

"Tarring a highway in 90-degree heat is hard work," says Todd. "This is baseball. Something I love. There's work that goes into being good at this. But work in the traditional sense of the word?"

No way!

Todd helps break ground on a new public sports complex. He tries to give more than his time to worthy causes—in this case he donated part of his salary so the project could get off to a quick start.

Index

PAGE NUMBERS IN ITALICS REFER TO ILLUSTRATIONS.